THE LOST SKETCH

THE LOST SKETCH

Andrea and David Spalding

Whitecap Books
Toronto/Vancouver

Copyright © 1999 by Brandywine Enterprises B.C. Ltd.
Whitecap Books
Vancouver/Toronto/New York

Edited by Lori Burwash
Proofread by Elizabeth McLean
Cover design by Susan Greenshields
Interior design by Antonia Banyard
Typeset by Tanya Lloyd
Calligraphy by Vivienne Wong
Printed in Canada

Canadian Cataloguing in Publication Data

Spalding, David A.E., 1937–
  The lost sketch

   (Adventure-net ; 1)
   ISBN 1-55110-989-1

   1. Art—Juvenile fiction. 2. Art dealers—Juvenile fiction. I. Spalding,
Andrea. II. Title. III. Series.
PS8587.P22138L67 1999   jC813'.54   C99-019833-6
PZ7.S7336Lo 1999

The publisher acknowledges the support of the Canada Council for the Arts
and the Cultural Services Branch of the Government of British Columbia for
our publishing program. We acknowledge the financial support of the
Government of Canada through the Book Industry Development Program for
our publishing activities.

Note to educators: A Teacher's Guide is available for this book.

For Anthony...
whose birthday fell on the day
we finished the story!

ACKNOWLEDGMENTS

The authors would like to thank Antonia Banyard for first approaching us with the series idea and Lori Burwash, our patient and encouraging editor.

Research assistance was provided at the Art Gallery of Ontario by Judith Mastai and Dennis Reid, and at the McMichael Canadian Art Collection by Megan Bice and Linda Morita. Other information was supplied by Jean Attisha, Susanne McRoberts and Terry Raybould, and Dr. Ron Jobe also made valuable suggestions. Many thanks to you all.

Special thanks goes to John O'Brian, Professor of Art History at the University of British Columbia, who not only provided Andrea with a wonderful personal tour of the AGO Group of Seven exhibit, but also read and commented on the draft text.

CHAPTER ONE

The day was blazing hot and picture perfect, but mutiny was in the air. The clear blue sky and brilliant sun made the northern Ontario lake sparkle and dance, but the occupants of the brightly coloured canoes were sweaty and cross.

"Aw, come on, Mr. Grantham, we've been paddling for ages."

Rick Forster laid his paddle across the canoe. "I'm on strike ... it's too hot."

"Right on, Rick," agreed his sister, Willow. "This is nuts. We didn't come all the way up to Algoma to die of heat stroke." She laid her paddle down and folded her arms.

The leader looked around. "This *is* canoe camp," he huffed, but trailed off when he realized that all the paddlers were following the Forsters' lead and pointedly putting down their paddles.

"Rotten kids. They need ten laps around the camp," Mr. Grantham muttered under his breath. He scanned the rocky shoreline, then cupped his hands and bellowed across the lake.

"All right, all right . . . head for that beach . . . take a break, cool off, and have some lunch."

A ragged cheer disturbed the peace. The paddlers dug into the water with renewed bursts of energy and glided towards the bay.

"Hey, thanks, guys." A tall boy walked over to Rick and Willow's yellow canoe. "It's hard to say anything to a leader like Mr. Grantham. That was gutsy." He slapped their hands in high fives.

"I'm Kassim. That's my paddling partner, Addid." A smaller boy looked up from stowing his paddle in a red canoe and waved.

"We're Rick and Willow Forster." Rick unfastened his life jacket and dropped it on the canoe seat. "We live on the west coast, but we're in Ontario for the summer."

"Yeah, our parents are working for three months in Toronto, so they thought canoe camp was a good idea. It keeps us out of their hair for a week," Willow explained. The three kids rolled their eyes at one another and giggled.

"Oh boy, will I be glad to get *in* the water instead of *on* it." Willow took a swig from her water bottle, dumped her backpack and life jacket in the shade, and ran and flopped into the lake.

"Aaaah, heaven." Scooping up a handful of cold water, she ran back and flung it over Rick and Kassim. "Who's up for a swim?"

Yelling, the boys abandoned the canoes and charged down the beach to retaliate.

The paddlers alternated between cooling off in the water and lazing in the shade. No one seemed to be in a hurry to continue the journey up the lake.

>>>>>>>>>>>>>>>>>> **W h e r e   i s   A l g o m a ?** <<<<<<<<<<<<<<<<<

 Algoma is a wild area north of Lake Superior in Ontario, several hundred kilometres northwest of Toronto.

"There are beautiful waterfalls on all sides, and the finest trees," said one early traveller into the Algoma district.

For hundreds of years, Algoma's beauty was appreciated only by First Peoples and fur traders. Then iron ores were found. Early in the twentieth century, a railway was built through the Algoma forests to take the ore south to the lakeside town of Sault Ste. Marie.

The Algoma landscape was made famous after 1918, when a small group of Canadian painters travelled up on the railway and began to paint the area. Later those painters became known as the Group of Seven. Now the region is a popular tourist destination, attracting visitors interested in both the railway and the wild country.

www.algoma.com/history.html

>><<<<<<<<<<<<<<<<<<<<<<<<<<<<<<<<<<<<<

Mr. Grantham decided to rethink the afternoon activities.

"OK, gang. You have a choice. We can continue up to the head of the lake, or we can stay here, practise our orienteering and mapping skills, and head back to camp when it's a little cooler. Who wants to continue up lake?"

The paddlers looked at one another slyly. Not a hand was raised.

"OK, we stay here." The leader took off his hat, bent down and filled it with water and poured it over his head. "Good choice."

Each mapping team took a compass reading and set out to explore a section of forest.

Willow and Rick surveyed their options. They could follow one of the trails that headed into their portion of woods, or they could map the area along the beach and over the rocky point.

"Sun or shade?" asked Rick.

Willow grinned, flicked her fair braids over her shoulders, and headed for the deepest patch of woodland.

The narrow deer trail was dappled with shadows. It was much cooler than the beach. Rick and Willow walked along slowly, jotting down the direction of a small trickle of water cutting across the path and the location of a burnt, scarred tree trunk.

"There must have been a lightning strike or an old forest fire," Rick said, making notes on his clipboard.

Willow nodded, a bit distracted. She was scraping her runner over something embedded in the dirt.

"Rick, look at this. It's a rail." She bent down and brushed away more dirt. "Two of them . . . It looks like an old railway line."

Rick bounded over. "Great!" He carefully marked the tracks down on his clipboard. "How did you spot them? They're covered with twigs and leaves."

"The ground just felt different when I stepped on it," Willow explained. She looked around. "No trains have been this way for ages." She gestured towards the trees. "You can barely tell where the line goes."

The two children looked. They could see a faint gap through the forest, where bushes and saplings grew instead of full-grown trees.

"Come on, let's follow the line." Willow pushed her way through the bushes. "It must go somewhere."

"Like an old logging or mining camp," suggested Rick. He followed her but had to duck smartly as a thin branch whipped back. "Hey, watch it! That branch almost took my eye out."

"Don't follow so close then," snapped Willow, and promptly stopped.

Rick cannoned into her. "Idiot!"

"No . . . Look!"

Almost hidden by young birches and a thicket of bushes stood the remains of a boxcar. Its sides were grey, warped and spotted with patches of peeling red paint and a few faint identification numbers. The wheels were clogged with grasses and creepers. The door hung at an angle, half off the runners, and the roof sagged—but the boxcar was occupied.

Willow pointed.

Two swallows swooped through the doorway, each carrying something in its beak. A moment later, they re-appeared.

"There must be a nest," whispered Rick.

Willow nodded. "I think I can hear babies chirping."

They edged through the undergrowth, up to the sagging doorway, and leaned inside.

The interior was dim, and their eyes took awhile to adjust.

The parent swallows twittered anxiously and circled around the doorway. Rick and Willow stayed quiet and still.

The calls of the young swallows intensified, and eventually the parents decided the children weren't a threat and flew inside.

When she spotted the nest, Willow covered her mouth to stop herself from laughing out loud.

A small mud cup, attached where the wall met the ceiling, was bursting at the seams with six young swallows. They oozed over the side like toothpaste squeezing out of a tube. Their mouths opened and shut and their cries were insistent and demanding. Their parents hesitated, then ignored the two children and flew frantically in and out, stuffing flies into their young.

"This place is cool." Rick clambered inside.

Willow wriggled up and followed him. "Someone's lived here. Look at the beds."

The sagging frames of two sets of bunk beds were nailed to the far wall. A small iron stove sat in a corner beside some wooden shelves.

The children scuffed through the piles of dead leaves on the floor. Rick kicked an old brandy bottle and it skittered around noisily. He looked up guiltily at the nest, but the birds ignored him.

Willow picked up a cracked plate from under a bunk. It was covered with splotches of paint, some swirled and mixed together. "An artist stayed here. This plate's been used as a palette."

She looked around thoughtfully. "The Group of Seven used a boxcar for painting trips in this part of Ontario. I learned about it in my art class." Willow turned excitedly to Rick and gestured around the boxcar. "Hey! What if this is it?"

Rick, busy climbing up the end of the bunk beds, only shrugged.

"Yeah right. We've just happened to discover the boxcar used by the most famous painters in Canada. Come on,

Willow... get real! It wouldn't have been left out here in the bush."

Rick tucked his feet under the top bar and hung upside down. The beds creaked in protest and pulled away from the wall. Rick dropped onto his hands and flipped upright.

"Great, wreck the place," Willow muttered, trying to push the bed frame back.

"Hold it." Rick peered through the gloom under the bunks. "Something's dropped." He stretched beneath the frame and pulled out a small rectangular board covered with dust and cobwebs. He wiped his sleeve over it and held it up towards the light. "It's painted."

"Let me see." Willow snatched it out of Rick's hand and ran to a patch of sunlight coming in through the doorway. She spat on the bottom of her tank top and wiped it lightly over the board.

Trees and a lake appeared.

Rick looked over her shoulder. "What a piece of junk," he laughed.

Willow shook with excitement. "Junk nothing! It's a sketch, a rough oil sketch—and it's good." She danced around the boxcar. "I bet this is it, Rick—I know it. What if this really is the boxcar used by the Group of Seven... and we've found one of their paintings?"

›››**What was the Group of Seven?**‹‹‹

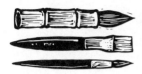 Early in the 1900s, several young Canadian painters created a scandal. At a time when Canadian art collectors preferred European landscapes full of cows, these painters travelled to northern Ontario and painted wilderness scenes in strong, bright colours. In some circles, their work was very unpopular. One critic even said it was "more like a . . . gob of porridge than a work of art."

Gradually their paintings found a following, and in 1920 they held their first group show, which included pictures of the Algoma region. They named themselves "the Group of Seven."

It was many years before the Group of Seven were widely accepted in the Canadian art world, but there were collectors who bought their work, and the National Gallery supported their activities. By the time of their last joint show, in 1931, they were regarded as Canada's leading painters. Now they are so famous that reproductions of their pictures can be seen in schools and other public buildings across Canada.

www.groupofsevenart.com
http://national.gallery.ca/virtual_tour/gallery109.html
http://national.gallery.ca/slidekits/groupof7/english/
content/content.html

CHAPTER TWO

Rick looked at Willow in astonishment, then grabbed the board from her and carried it to the doorway. He sat on the floor, legs dangling over the edge, and tilted the board towards the sunlight. He shook his head in disbelief. "You're losing it. No way was this done by a famous artist."

Willow moved behind him and looked over his shoulder. "I've just taken art classes at the Art Gallery of Ontario, right?"

Rick nodded. "Yeah . . . so now you're an expert?"

Willow shoved him. "Shut up and listen."

Rick grinned, but moved over so Willow could sit down.

"We didn't just paint in the classroom. We looked at paintings in the galleries. Some were by the Group of Seven. We saw a whole bunch of their sketches. Rough paintings on small boards like this. They all looked kind of messy. Turn this one over."

Rick flipped the board.

"See, it's not a real artist's board."

"It's just a piece of wood," agreed Rick.

"Right. The Group of Seven painted on small cedar boards or bits of packing cases...cheap stuff. Then they took the sketches home and did a big painting later, sometimes years later."

Rick whipped out his pencil and dotted something on the back of the shingle.

"Hey, stop it! What are you doing?"

Laughing, Rick showed Willow a small knot in the grain of the wood. He'd added two eyes and a mouth, so a tiny impish face grinned back at them.

Shocked, Willow snatched the board out of his hands.

"Knock it off, Rick! What if this is worth money?"

"So what. Who'd notice?"

Willow snorted, but turned the board over and looked closely at the painting. "Know what? I think this is the shoreline near where we landed." She eagerly pointed to a detail. "See the rock in the front? It's just like the one we had to avoid."

Rick grinned lazily. "OK, so first you find a Group of Seven painting and now you know exactly where it was painted!" He slid down from the boxcar and picked up his clipboard. "Come on, give me the compass reading from the boxcar back down the line. We should be going."

"You don't believe me, do you?" Willow's cheeks flushed with frustration.

"You've got to admit it sounds pretty crazy. The sketch is

probably by that artist from the village. Bet he was sketching here, then dumped it because it was no good. Come on...are you going to give me that compass reading or not?"

"Do it yourself." Willow tossed the compass at Rick. It bounced off his clipboard and into a patch of nettles.

Swearing, Rick dragged it out with the corner of his clipboard. He noted the reading on his paper, then stalked down the rail line without looking back.

The boxcar trips

In spring 1918, artist Lawren Harris went with his friend Dr. MacCallum to northern Ontario. Harris was looking for new landscape to paint and fell in love with the dramatic country along the Algoma Railway. He was able to arrange for a boxcar to be made available so that a group of his fellow artists could also paint the landscape.

During 1918 and 1919, several artists spent a few weeks each year in the boxcar. Every day they explored the country on foot or by canoe. Sometimes they rode along the tracks in a speeder—a three-wheeled wagon powered by a lever hinged in the middle, like a teeter-totter. When they found sites they wanted to paint, they would settle down to work. Every few days, a locomotive came by to move the car to another location.

Silence fell.

Willow looked at the oil sketch again, then clambered to her feet. She walked around the interior of the boxcar once more, hugging the painting to her chest.

"I know I'm right," she whispered to herself. "I can feel it." She looked carefully around, committing everything to memory—the way the bunks were built, the stove, the shelves, even the brandy bottle and plate. "This *is* important, but I'll have to prove it. I'll show Rick . . . I'll show everyone . . ."

Willow lifted the back of her tank top and carefully wedged the board between the waistband of her shorts and her spine. The loose material from her top fell down, concealing all the edges. She gave one last glance around.

"Bye, swallows," she called. "You're growing up in a famous place." Then she leapt from the boxcar and ran to catch up with Rick.

The evening din in Camp Hiawatha's rec room was steadily rising. A group of kids was dancing at one end, a table tennis game was in full swing at the other. The TV blared out videos to no one in particular, and Willow was fighting off kids from the computer.

"Come on, Willow. Just one game," wheedled Addid.

"Forget it. Your last game took two hours. This is the first time I've been on the computer since camp started."

Willow ignored Addid's begging and concentrated on her Web research.

Rick looked across the room at his sister. No one would ever have guessed they were brother and sister. He was dark, she was fair. He was short, she was tall. He never understood what made her tick. Like him, she was good at sports, but unlike him, she didn't like being part of a team. She'd rather lie around reading or doodling in her sketch book. The big thing they had in common was the computer. They were both whizzes at it. Rick smiled as he watched Addid try to con Willow into playing a computer game with him. He'd regret it—she'd slaughter him. But Rick knew Addid may as well quit bugging her. Once Willow had started surfing it would take a bomb blast to break her concentration.

Rick played hackysack for a while, then wandered over to see what she'd found.

"Hi, sis. Whatcha doing?"

Willow turned red and hunched closer to the screen.

Rick looked over her shoulder. "AGO—Art Gallery of Ontario—You researching that Group of Seven stuff?"

"Shhh," said Willow urgently, "don't make a public announcement." She signed off and looked seriously at Rick. "We've got to talk."

"OK, let's sit on the dock."

"Hey, Rick, Willow, want to try and beat me and Maria?

We're rockin'!" yelled Kassim from across the room, waving a table tennis paddle.

"Later," Rick answered.

Kassim waved an OK and turned his attention back to the game. Rick and Willow slid through the door and ran across the grass to the deserted dock.

The air was silky but still not cool, even though the sun was almost below the horizon. The few gold-lined clouds floating in a pink sky were reflected by Lake Gitche Gumee. Hundreds of dragonflies flew over the water, competing with the fish for insects.

Willow lay down on her stomach and hung over the edge of the dock. "There's a school of tiny fish around the pilings."

Rick flopped down beside her and they watched in silence for a while.

"So . . ." Rick looked sideways at Willow. "You still mad at me? You were real quiet paddling to camp."

"No, I'm not still mad . . . but you can be a jerk sometimes. No, I was just thinking—and my back was sore."

"How come?"

" 'Cause I had that painting stuck in my shorts and it was rubbing me."

Rick snorted. "You never give up, do you! Why hide it?"

Willow scratched her nose, thinking. "Not sure . . . I guess because it might be famous and I felt kind of weird taking it. Like, was it stealing?"

Rick rolled on his back. "I dunno. Finders keepers, I guess." He looked at Willow again. "Do you really think it's worth something?"

"Guess so, if it is by someone important. And I think it is."

"How do we find out for sure?"

"Show it to someone who might know." Willow hesitated. "But I don't want to take it to the AGO in case it's no good. People might laugh, like you did."

Rick looked slightly ashamed. "Sorry. But it does seem pretty crazy."

"Yeah?" said Willow defensively. "Well, crazy things happen sometimes. People are always finding valuable things in attics, or buying a Picasso sketch in a junk store. Why shouldn't we find something in a broken-down old boxcar? I think it is the real boxcar. I researched on the Web about the Group of Seven. There's even a description of it and a number we can check out."

"OK, OK . . . I said I'm sorry. Where's the painting now?"

"In my locker, wrapped in a sweater."

"You could wait until Mom and Dad pick us up on Sunday. They'd help."

"It's only Tuesday. . . Sunday is ages away." Willow turned onto her elbow to face Rick. "It's our free afternoon tomorrow. Do you want to come with me? We'll find that artist in the village, see if he can help."

"OK . . . but only if we can get ice cream on the way."

"Deal!"

Willow ran to her cabin. It was empty; Maria and her other cabinmates were still hanging out in the rec room. She opened her locker, lifted her folded clothes, and pulled out the sweater-wrapped oil sketch. She sat on the side of her bed, removed the sweater, and gazed at the sketch.

She remembered her art teacher talking about works by the Group. *Bold colours and vigorous brush strokes give the sketch energy and rhythm.* Even though the sketch was dirty, its colours hinted at a fall day in Ontario's north country.

No, I'm not crazy, Willow decided. *This is good.* She scanned the strong lines of the tree trunks and traced the rocks lightly with her fingers. *Wish I could paint like this,* she thought. *I wonder which Group of Seven artist did it?*

Her mind ran over everything she could remember. Who went on the boxcar trips? Lawren Harris did for sure, because he organized them. But who else?

A peal of laughter warned Willow that Maria was coming. She quickly slid the painting under her clean clothes, locked the door, and stretched out on her bed, a book in hand.

"Group of Seven" now seems an odd name for these artists because at different times there were actually ten of them! The original seven members (each with the name of one of his most famous paintings) were:

- Franklin Carmichael (*Jackfish Village*)
- Lawren Harris (*Above Lake Superior*)
- A.Y. Jackson (*The Red Maple*)
- Franz Johnston (*Fire Swept, Algoma*)
- Arthur Lismer (*September Gale, Georgian Bay*)
- J.E.H. MacDonald (*The Tangled Garden*)
- F.H. Varley (*Stormy Weather, Georgian Bay*)

Johnston resigned before the group broke up, and artists who joined the group later were:

- A.J. Casson (*White Pine*)
- L.L. Fitzgerald (*Doc Snider's House*)
- Edwin Holgate (*Melting Snow*)

Other artists strongly associated with the group, but never members, were:

- Tom Thomson—his style inspired the members, but he died before the group was formed.
- Emily Carr—she painted the west coast in a similar way, but was never asked to join.

www.tomthomson.org/g7room.htm

CHAPTER THREE

Willow and Rick wandered through the summer village of MacCallum, licking the drips off their ice cream cones. It was crowded. Tourists visiting Group of Seven country mingled with fishers stocking up on supplies and kids from Camp Hiawatha. The mood was festive, with fluttering flags, a musician busking, and families picnicking and playing ball beside the lake.

"I think the art studio is near the car park," said Willow, looking up and down Main Street. "I remember passing it on the way to camp."

The two kids headed up Main Street, dodged around groups of shoppers, crossed the street, and finally stood in front of the art studio's small wooden gate.

Willow nudged Rick. "Notice the name?"

Rick looked at the sign, "Tangled Garden Gallery," and then over the gate to the tiny yard and the mass of flowers and ornamental grasses spilling out of flower beds, window boxes, and pots.

"It's named after a well-known Group of Seven

painting —*The Tangled Garden* by J.E.H. MacDonald."

Rick looked admiringly at Willow. "You really do know your stuff, don't you?"

Willow thumped his shoulder. "I like my art classes."

>>>>>>>>>>>>>> **S h o c k i n g   s u n f l o w e r s** <<<<<<<<<<<<<

Giant sunflowers bend over a riot of red flowers in a garden of many shades of green. *The Tangled Garden* is based on J.E.H. MacDonald's own gardens near his home in Thornhill, Ontario. It is one of his most famous paintings.

The Tangled Garden was first exhibited in 1916 with other paintings by MacDonald, but many people criticized the show. One critic called *The Tangled Garden* "an experimental painting" and said that another picture looked like "Hungarian goulash or a Drunkard's Stomach."

For more than twenty years, MacDonald was unable to sell his colourful painting. Finally, it was purchased in 1939 and presented to the National Gallery of Canada. It is now one of MacDonald's best-loved works.

http://national.gallery.ca/slidekits/groupof7/english/
slide-gallery/slide3.html

>>><<<<<<<<<<<<<<<<<<<<<<<<<<<<<<<<<<<

Willow pushed open the gate and Rick followed her down the path. She paused in the open doorway of a small cottage.

A bell rang.

"Come on in. Come on in. Look around . . . I'll be with you in a moment," called a deep cheerful voice from behind a folding screen.

Rick and Willow peered curiously around the room. The walls were covered with small oil paintings, but there was also a cabinet displaying artist's supplies and some "How to Draw" books.

The paintings seemed vaguely familiar. Willow looked closely at one of a stream with some red fall leaves floating in the water, and another showing a dark pine tree silhouetted against the blue waters of a distant lake.

A older bearded man stepped around the divider, wiping his hands on a pungent rag. "I'm halfway through an oil painting," he apologized. "Just let me get the smudges off my fingers." He finished wiping his hands, dumped the rag on the corner of a half-hidden table, and turned towards them with a smile.

"Welcome to Tangled Garden Gallery. I'm Kristo. How can I help? Looking for a gift for someone?"

Willow shook her head. "Not exactly. We—we were wondering . . . " She trailed off. This wasn't going to be easy.

"Like, we need some information," Rick blurted out.

"About the Group of Seven," finished Willow with a rush.

The man looked at their matching red shorts sporting the camp logo and laughed. "Doing a project are you? At one of the camps? Well, you've come to the right place."

He gestured to the paintings on the walls. "The Group of Seven are my heroes. No one has ever painted better than them. I copy the way they painted. I paint the same subjects and use the same methods and techniques." He laughed. "I even use the same colours. Why try to improve on perfection, eh?"

Willow looked at the paintings again. "So that's why these are kinda familiar. They're copies of famous paintings?"

Kristo closed his eyes and grimaced as if in pain. "Not 'copies,' my dear. These are originals . . . *My* originals. What I like to call 'School of Group of Seven.'"

"Do you go out and paint from life like they did?" asked Willow.

"Not really," Kristo acknowledged. "I did when I was younger, but the wilderness isn't exactly my thing." He shivered dramatically. "Not too keen on wolves and bears, you know."

Rick and Willow grinned.

"No," Kristo continued. "I study their work daily, then paint from their inspiration. They never fail me." He clasped his hands together and cast his eyes heavenward. "Soul mates, that's what we are . . . soul mates."

"Do you own any Group of Seven paintings?" asked Rick curiously.

Kristo laughed. "Goodness gracious, I wish, I wish. No, I study their work from books and make do with occasional visits to the Art Gallery of Ontario and the McMichael to pay homage."

"What about the boxcar? Did you ever paint from there?" asked Willow.

"The Group of Seven's boxcar? That's long gone," Kristo said.

Rick nudged Willow. "Are you going to show him?"

Willow looked uncomfortable, but she wriggled her backpack off her shoulders. Opening the flap, she lifted out the sweater-swathed bundle, peeled back the wrapping, and held up the shingle.

"What have we here?" Kristo looked from the shingle to the children.

"We found it. In a beat-up boxcar. On the old railway line that runs along the lake," Willow said hesitantly.

Rick jumped in. "I think it was done by a local artist, like you, but Willow thinks it's a real Group of Seven sketch."

Kristo gave a deep chuckle. "Hoping to make your fortunes, are you? Come on, let's take a look."

He disappeared around the screen. The children followed and found themselves in his studio. A half-finished painting of another lake and trees sat on an easel by a large window. A table covered with tubes of paint, a jar of brushes, rags, and turpentine was close at hand. Kristo marched past the table to a desk in the corner. He switched on a lamp and trained the beam on the shingle.

"Hmm . . . nice little oil sketch." Kristo paused for a long time looking at it, chewing his cheek. "Could be an early one of mine," he said eventually.

"Told you," whispered Rick to Willow.

She shot a dagger-like look at him and stomped on his foot.

There was another pause while Kristo looked even more closely at the sketch. He opened a drawer, pulled out a magnifying glass, and peered at the sketch yet again. "Where did you say you found it?" he asked, puzzled.

"In an old boxcar. We canoed up the lake, and went exploring," explained Rick.

Kristo looked at the painting in his hand, flipped it to note the wooden back, and turned again to the painted side. "Ah yes," he said faintly, "the spur line . . . the old boxcar on the spur line . . . I remember now . . . the one on the northwest bank of the lake, was it?"

Willow looked at him oddly. "Is there more than one boxcar?"

Kristo rubbed his forehead as if to clear it, switched off the light and changed the subject.

"Of course, this is pretty dirty," he said briskly. "It needs cleaning before we can really see what it is. Why don't you leave it with me for a few days? When are you back in the village?"

"Our parents pick us up on Sunday," suggested Rick. "Are you open then?"

>>>>>>>>>>>>>>>>>>>>>>> **Oil painting** <<<<<<<<<<<<<<<<<<<<<

 Have you ever painted with oil paints? It's like painting with coloured mud. Oil paints are made of pigments (coloured substances) mixed with linseed oil. Artists often mix them on an oval palette, but any flat surface will do— like an old plate. Then they use a brush or palette knife to paint the picture on a canvas or board. Oil paint dries slowly and stays soft long enough to be reworked as the painting develops.

In the past, artists such as Leonardo da Vinci and Michelangelo often had young assistants to grind and mix the colours—one shade of brown was produced from powdered Egyptian mummies. The Group of Seven artists were among the first who could buy paints ready-made in tubes, making it possible to paint outdoors. All the members painted in oils. Some of them also used other techniques, including watercolour, engraving, and drawing.

www.arts.ufl.edu/art/rt_room/@rtroom_doorway.html
www.kidzdraw.com

"I'm open every day in the summer, till late in the evening," replied Kristo ruefully. "Got to make a living, you know. Sure, come back Sunday."

"I—er—thought cleaning paintings was a special job," said Willow uneasily.

"Indeed it is." Kristo bent down and pulled out a painting leaning against the wall. Half of it was so dark it was impossible to see any features. The other half had been cleaned, and a picture of a shepherdess with sheep was emerging.

"This is what I do in the winter, clean and restore old paintings. Everyone thinks they have a Rembrandt in their attic." Kristo smiled at Willow. "I won't damage your painting. Just give it a light clean to remove the surface dirt. Trust me?"

Willow nodded slowly but looked uncertain. "Maybe I shouldn't leave it."

"If it's a valuable painting, you don't want it hanging around camp, do you? It should be locked up."

Willow still looked undecided.

"Tell you what," Kristo suggested. "We'll make this official." He opened a drawer and pulled out a pad of receipts.

The kids looked at each other in alarm.

"It's OK. We'll just take it away—show it to our parents," said Willow hurriedly.

"Yeah . . . Keep it as a souvenir of our trip," agreed Rick.

Kristo looked at them with a twinkle. "No money, eh?" The kids looked embarrassed. "It's all right. I'm not going to charge you."

"Here." Kristo scribbled a note on the pad and looked up again. "What are your names?"

"Willow and Rick Forster," muttered Willow, feeling trapped and wishing she'd never come.

Kristo added their names, tore the receipt off the pad, handed it to Willow, and briskly ushered the kids to the door.

"There. It's all official. I'll lock the painting up safely. Bye, see you on Sunday."

Rick and Willow somehow found themselves out on the sidewalk. Willow clutched the receipt in one hand and her backpack in the other.

"This doesn't feel right. He's too weird." She looked at the receipt. "We shouldn't have left the sketch. Do you think he's lying?"

"Don't know," admitted Rick. "But I don't think he knew about the boxcar."

"Me neither," agreed Willow. "*Now* what do we do?"

The two looked back at the studio just in time to see the cottage door shut firmly and a hand put a "CLOSED" sign in the window.

CHAPTER FOUR

Kristo sat at his desk clenching his fists. "I don't believe it," he muttered to himself. "After all these years of devoting myself to the style of the Group of Seven, what might be the real thing is brought in by a couple of kids." He thumped the desk hard. "It's cruel...that's what it is...cruel."

He picked up the oil sketch and looked at it closely. "What a little beauty," he whispered. He gazed at the painting thoughtfully. "That Willow kid is smart, but she's just guessing."

He sighed, carefully placed the sketch in a plastic bag, and locked it in the desk drawer. Then he began tapping his fingers on the desk.

Hmm...a boxcar on the old spur line, he thought. *Could it really be? If it is, are any more sketches kicking around?*

"Closed! He said he was open every day," spluttered Willow.

"Till late," added Rick.

"So why suddenly close, the minute he gets his hands on my painting?"

"Hi, guys," called Maria, "you look bummed. What's up?" Maria and Kassim crossed the street to join them.

"Willow's wondering if she's been ripped off," admitted Rick.

"How come?" asked Maria.

"Can't tell you," muttered Willow.

"Come on, Willow. You could use some help. Maria and Kassim won't say anything, will you?"

Mystified, Maria and Kassim promised.

Willow gave in. "OK, but let's keep an eye on the art studio."

The four friends trooped down the street to a small park and sat in the shade of an old maple. Willow kept her eyes fixed on the studio gate.

"What gives?" asked Kassim, bursting with curiosity.

The whole story came pouring out.

Maria looked back thoughtfully at the studio, then across to Kassim. "Why don't Willow and Rick stay here. We'll take a walk down the alley and check it out, see if anything's happening at the back of the studio. Kristo doesn't know us, so it won't matter if we're seen."

Kassim jumped up and pulled Maria to her feet. They sauntered over to the corner of the next street and disappeared.

It seemed like ages before they returned.

"Guess what?" Maria bubbled. "He's going on a hike!"

"What?" Willow exchanged a look with Rick.

"Yeah—he's loading up a backpack," explained Kassim. "We could see it on the table through a big window. We stood talking in the alley, and he came out to the shed and went back to the cottage with a flashlight. Then he stuffed it in the backpack."

"I get it! He's going to find the boxcar," said Willow with conviction.

"Bet you're right," said Rick. "But why in such a hurry?"

"Because I really *did* find a Group of Seven," said Willow positively. "And he wants to see if there are any more."

"Let's follow him?" suggested Kassim.

"Cool idea," exclaimed Rick. He thought for a moment. "The railway cuts through the middle of the village, right?"

Everyone nodded.

"And the spur line we found followed the lakeshore?"

Willow nodded again.

"So the start of the spur line must be close by. If that's where Kristo goes, we'll know for sure he's heading for the boxcar."

"If Rick and Willow watch the front gate again, and we go to spy at the back . . . " Maria trailed off. "Uh-oh, here he comes—Don't look, you idiots!" she whispered furiously as everyone started to turn. "Play it cool."

Willow, Rick, and Kassim sat riveted to the spot as

Maria gave a blow-by-blow account of Kristo's movements. "He's closed the gate ... He's looking up and down the street." She bent her head and shifted slightly so Kristo wouldn't see her.

"OK ... he's heading towards the edge of town."

Keeping their distance and making sure other people were always between them and Kristo, the four friends followed.

Kristo walked briskly up the road, then suddenly turned into the trees and vanished.

The children speeded up to find the same spot.

"It's a hiking trail." Willow got excited. "There's a map of all the hiking trails in the centre of town. We'll be able to figure out where he's going."

They raced back into the village and stopped breathlessly in front of the large map.

Willow traced the road out of town with her finger and stopped at a big number 3. "What does it say for trail three, Rick?"

Rick read from the side of the board. "An easy four-kilometre loop trail that cuts over the promontory, then levels out along the lakeshore using the bed of an old spur line from the Algoma Central Railway. After two kilometres, the trail reaches a small canyon containing a spectacular waterfall and the remains of an old trestle bridge. From this point, the trail loops back through the forest. The trestle is dangerous, so visitors are warned not to venture beyond the trailhead."

Willow yipped with delight. "That's it! That's why the boxcar is still there. It couldn't get back over the bridge."

>>>>>>> **A railway in the wilderness** <<<<

The artists who later formed the Group of Seven wanted to paint wilderness, and one of the few places they could easily visit it was along the Algoma Central Railway (A.C.R.) in northern Ontario. The A.C.R. was built between 1899 and 1914 to transport iron ore south for smelting in Sault Ste. Marie.

The railway was built through wild landscapes of rocks, lakes, and rivers, and had to cross many creeks and canyons. Wooden trestle bridges were constructed, but the local trees were too small, so logs had to be brought in from British Columbia.

Paintings by the Group of Seven artists made the Algoma landscape famous, and now people want to see the wilderness area they painted. The railway still runs 476 km from Sault Ste. Marie to Hearst, stopping at stations with names such as Canyon, Hubert, and Batchewana. It mainly carries freight, but tourists can take a day trip with a stop at Agawa Canyon, or an overnight "Tour of the Line."

www.sault-Canada.com/tourism-attractions-agawa.htm
www.soonet.ca/publibrary/pages/photoacr.htm

"Oh boy! So Kristo has to go over the trestle? Why didn't he rent a boat?" asked Maria.

"He doesn't know how to find the boxcar from the lake," said Rick. "All he knows is that it's somewhere on the spur line."

"I wish we had a power boat," Willow said wistfully. "Then we could get there before Kristo does."

"There's one at camp—but you've gotta be over twelve and have a Power Squadron certificate before you can sign it out," said Rick. He moodily kicked a loose rock.

"That's me!" Kassim grinned.

CHAPTER FIVE

The four friends stood impatiently on the dock, going through the paperwork with Mr. Grantham.

"You all have life jackets?" Mr. Grantham ran his eyes over the group, then ticked his form.

"You have a Power Squadron certificate, Kassim?"

"Come on, sir... you know I do," Kassim groaned.

Mr. Grantham grinned. "Just teasing. OK, Kassim, do your fuel check."

Kassim leapt on board and checked the outboard motor and the extra fuel container. "Looks good, sir."

Mr. Grantham eyed them all sternly. "No fooling around, and don't go farther up the lake than a half-hour run. Be back by six."

Willow, Rick, and Maria stepped into the boat. Kassim started the motor as Willow unhooked the bow rope and coiled it neatly.

"Ready? Catch," called Mr. Grantham, flinging the stern rope.

Rick caught the rope and stowed it. Kassim swung the

boat away from the dock, and they were off, skimming lightly over the water.

"Wheeeee," laughed Willow, spreading her arms wide to catch the cool breeze whipping past them.

"Think you'll recognize the beach?" Maria shouted.

Willow nodded. "I remember the point and the tree, and the big rock in the water."

Maria turned to watch the shoreline, the wind whipping her dark hair behind her.

"This is a blast!" Rick shouted over the roar of the motor.

Kassim agreed. "We'll have to make sure we don't whiz past the beach though. It seemed a long way when we were paddling into all the little bays, but it didn't take us that long to canoe straight back."

"Can you get closer to the shore?" called Willow. "The canyon with the waterfall and trestle should be coming up."

Kassim slowed down and edged closer to the shore. "I can't spot the rocks when the water is rough. This is as close as I'm going."

The mouth of the canyon opened up and the boat bobbed in the turbulent water.

The four friends looked up at the trestle bridge.

"Ugh," shuddered Maria. "I'm glad I'm not walking over it."

Willow agreed. "Yeah, look at those missing planks. No wonder you're not supposed to use it."

Kassim cranked the engine and the boat zoomed farther out into the lake. "Mr. Grantham said the beach we went to was about four kilometres up the lake. I wonder how fast Kristo walks."

"Maybe he's already there." Willow was anxious.

They cruised for a while in silence, intently watching the shoreline.

Suddenly Willow clutched Rick's arm. "Hey, look over there by those trees—can you see him?"

Rick looked through his binoculars.

"That person walking along the bluff."

Rick focused. "It's Kristo!"

"He'll see us. We're in plain view," said Maria uneasily.

"Naw, we're just a boat on the lake," Willow reassured her. "Why would he think it's us?"

"You're right. Bet the beach isn't far though." Maria resumed watching the shore.

The powerboat rounded a point and everyone spotted it at the same time—a beach with a small rocky headland and a distinctive lone pine.

A quiet cheer went up.

"We don't have much time, he's not far behind," Rick worried. "Do we anchor and swim in, or can we take the boat onto the beach?"

"Up to the beach," Kassim replied. "As long as you don't mind getting your feet wet." He cut the motor and waited for the boat to glide towards the gravel. He tipped the propeller out of the water and motioned the others to slip over the side.

"All clear. Pull her up," directed Kassim, leaning back to lift the bow.

"Heave," said Rick, and they pulled the boat partially onto the gravel.

Kassim jumped out and checked the boat's resting place. "Looks fine to me. Now what?"

"Come on—and keep it down. Let's get to the boxcar before Kristo. We'll hide in the forest and watch what he does." Willow led the way down the deer trail.

"Then what?" persisted Kassim.

Willow thought for a moment. "If he starts snooping around, we can spook him."

"How?" asked Maria.

Everyone stopped and looked at Willow.

Willow grinned at Rick. "Remember when we were in Kristo's studio?"

Rick nodded.

"Kristo said the wilderness wasn't really his thing."

Rick smirked. "Yeah. He said there were too many wolves and bears."

Willow's blue eyes danced. "And what did we do at campfire last night?"

"Wolf howl, wolf howl," everyone chanted quietly and burst out laughing.

"Shhhhhh . . . Kristo might hear us. We've gotta get to the boxcar." Willow jogged impatiently.

Muffling their giggles, the group followed Willow down the trail to the rail lines, then through the overgrown cut line to the boxcar.

>>>>>>>>>>>>>>>>>>> **H o w l   l i k e   a   w o l f** <<<<<<<<<<<<<<<

 Black bears and wolves are fairly common in Ontario forests, but Kristo doesn't really have much reason to be scared. Bears normally stay away from people unless attracted by unprotected food or garbage, and they will not usually attack unless people are close to their cubs.

Wolves are rarely seen, but can sometimes be heard howling. In some northern Ontario parks and other places where people and wolves share space, groups of people will get together at dusk and howl until the wolves howl back. This is a favourite campfire activity.

www.nature.ca/notebooks/english/wolf.htm
www.cws-scf.ec.gc.ca/hwww-fap/wolf/wolf.html
www.cws-scf.ec.gc.ca/hwww-fap/blbear/blbear.html

CHAPTER SIX

Kristo stopped to wipe the perspiration dripping off his forehead. The heat on the rocky bluff was incredible. It radiated up from the rocks and down from the sun. Maybe the shade was a better idea, even if the going was rougher.

Kristo walked to the nearest pine tree, sat in its shade and slumped against the trunk. He looked out over the lake, wishing he was on the small boat cruising past. "I sure hope that boxcar isn't much farther," he muttered to himself.

Kristo had been shaken by Willow's find, but now the hike was giving him time to think. *The Group of Seven!* All his life, Kristo had tried to live up to their image, but he didn't have enough talent. He could competently imitate their painting style, but he didn't possess one scrap of artistic originality. It was his biggest frustration.

And now a couple of scrawny kids had stumbled across what *might* be the greatest art discovery in years—not only what looked like a genuine sketch, but maybe the actual boxcar used by the Group of Seven. All practically on his doorstep.

Kristo broke out in another sweat just thinking about it.

Naw! Impossible! But . . . if the sketch is genuine . . . if the boxcar is genuine!

Kristo daydreamed happily for a few minutes. Kristo the official guide for tours to the boxcar. Kristo, the local Group of Seven expert. Kristo getting rich as his paintings of the boxcar sold by the thousands!

With renewed energy and optimism, Kristo clambered to his feet. He had to find the boxcar, verify it, and see if there were more sketches. If everything looked genuine, he then had to figure out how to hang on to Willow's sketch.

"Shouldn't be too difficult," he muttered under his breath. "After all, they are just a couple of camp kids. What do *they* know about art? Maybe they'll sell it to me if I tell the right story."

The wait for Kristo seemed to last forever. Mosquitoes began to find the children, and—not daring to make noise by slapping them—the kids were scratching. But suddenly they heard him, and the mosquitoes were forgotten.

Kristo was whistling.

Willow and Rick nudged each other as they lay under a bush. They were well concealed by the leafy branches from above and the long grass in front of their hiding place. They each parted a few strands to peek through.

Maria crouched behind an alder thicket, deep in the forest shadows. She was so still that a chickadee hopped within reach before flying off in confusion.

Kassim was perched high in a pine tree, lying along a branch. He grinned and gave the thumbs-up sign to Maria's shadowy form.

She waved back nervously, hoping he wouldn't fall.

Kristo pushed through the bushes and stood and stared.

"Halle - flaming - lujah," he exclaimed, "it's really here!"

A muffled snort escaped from under the bush, but Kristo was oblivious. He shrugged off his backpack, unzipped a pocket, and pulled out a piece of paper. He looked from the paper to the boxcar. "A red boxcar from the Algoma Central Railway," he read. He walked over to the boxcar and gently touched the patches of peeling red paint.

Kristo read from the paper again. "Number one ... " Reverently, he walked over to where remnants of black numbers were visible on the wooden boards. He traced the first number with his finger.

"Zero." He traced again.

"Five, five, seven," Kristo finished quickly. He staggered to the open doorway and sat down with a thump. He put his head in his hands as though he was dizzy.

"Holy cow," he gasped. "Holy, holy cow. This is it!"

Under the bush, Rick nudged Willow. "You were right," he whispered in her ear. "Sorry."

Willow stuck out her tongue and mouthed, "Told you so!"

>>>>>>>>>>>>>>>> **A s t u d i o o n w h e e l s** <<<<<<<<<<<<<<<

The Algoma Central Railway provided Lawren Harris and his friends with Boxcar A.C.R. 10557. "That figure became our street number on the long way of the wilderness," said MacDonald.

The boxcar was already equipped with bunks, chairs and a table, lamps, a cupboard, a water tank, a sink, and a stove. But like kids with a new room, the artists decorated their studio on wheels to suit their taste. They hung a Christmas tree over the main door and a moose skull under the window. On one wall, above a spray of evergreen branches and berries and their intertwined initials, they painted the Latin motto *Ars longa, vita brevis* ("Art is long, life is short").

The artists brought their painting materials, food, books, and ideas. After painting all day, they spent the evenings in the boxcar, sitting around the stove discussing art, philosophy, and religion late into the night.

>><<<<<<<<<<<<<<<<<<<<<<<<<<<<<<<<<<<<<<<<<

Dazedly shaking his head, Kristo stood and picked up his backpack. He put it in the doorway of the boxcar, unzipped it and pulled out his camera. He walked backwards into the clearing and took several photos of the boxcar. Then he returned the camera to his backpack, pulled out the flashlight, and clambered inside the boxcar. The children could hear him moving around.

Suddenly Kassim lobbed a pine cone. It landed on the roof of the boxcar, rolled across, and fell off one end. The noise inside the boxcar stopped.

Kassim lobbed another cone onto the roof. Kristo appeared in the doorway and looked around. "Must be squirrels." He shrugged and turned back inside.

Willow, Rick, and Maria watched with delight as Kassim tossed more pine cones onto the roof and into the bushes. They tumbled through the branches, making a rustling sound like an animal passing through.

Each time, Kristo appeared in the doorway and nervously looked around. Each time, when all was still, he returned to his search. The children could hear Kristo scrabbling and scraping, then a pile of leaves shot through the open door, followed by the brandy bottle. When the bottle hit the ground, Rick let out a couple of yips as though he were a startled dog. From behind the alders, Maria growled.

When Kristo reappeared in the doorway, Kassim howled and Willow joined in. The bloodcurdling noise rolled eerily around the clearing.

White-faced, Kristo leapt from the boxcar, grabbed his backpack, and fumbled inside it. He half crouched, his back to the boxcar, clutching a can of pepper spray in a shaky hand. He looked fearfully around the clearing.

Once again Willow howled. This time Rick, Maria, and Kassim joined in.

Kristo ran. The awful howls echoed behind him. He jumped over a small bush, pushed blindly through some saplings, and raced up the cut line, leaving nothing behind except a piece of paper fluttering in the grass.

The kids howled once more for good measure, then Willow, Rick, and Maria crawled out of their hiding places while Kassim swung down from the tree. After hitting high fives all around, they collapsed giggling on the ground.

"That cone idea was awesome," Willow bubbled. Kassim grinned proudly. "And Maria's growl was totally lifelike."

Laughing, the kids relived the prank.

"What was with the paper and the numbers?" asked Kassim.

Willow plucked the paper from the grass. She glanced at it and passed it around. "Kristo researched the same stuff I found on the Web last night. I saw a bunch of books about the Group of Seven at his studio. He must have quickly checked them before he left. This is a description of the boxcar, complete with the number." She pointed to the faint numbers on the side of the boxcar.

Maria got up and checked both sets of numbers. "So it's proof—you really *have* found a famous picture."

"Well . . . " Willow wrinkled her nose thoughtfully. "The boxcar is for real—but I dunno about the sketch. It isn't signed. It could have been done by anyone. But it sure looks like other Group of Seven sketches I've seen."

"How do you find out?" asked Maria.

"We'll check for more clues here, see what Kristo says, then go to the AGO when we get back to Toronto. I'll show it to my art teacher."

"Maria and I live in Toronto," said Kassim. "You've gotta let us know how it ends. We're part of your team, right?"

Rick and Willow grinned.

"Right. The four musketeers!" suggested Rick.

"Mosquitoes, more like," said Kassim.

Everyone giggled.

"Lame, Kassim, really lame," said Maria, shoving him.

"We don't have much time. Let's look for more paintings and clues." Willow climbed inside.

"Yeah, like the C.I.A.," said Rick, getting into the spirit of things.

"What kind of clues?" Maria looked unsure.

"Anything. Anything that might help us find out who used it," ordered Willow. "We'll take the clues back to camp."

"Like this?" Maria gingerly picked up the brandy bottle and placed it in the doorway.

"Yep, and this." Willow added the broken piece of paint-covered plate.

"Wish we'd brought a flashlight," muttered Kassim as he edged under the bunks and scraped debris out with a long stick. A rusted sardine can slid into view. "Do you want this?"

"Everything," said Willow firmly.

Kassim added it to the pile along with a flattened cigarette packet.

Rick rubbed his T-shirt sleeve over the small window to let in more light and wandered across to the stove. He looked underneath, opened the door, and poked inside. Nothing but a small pile of ashes. He coughed as the dust caught in his throat, and closed the door quickly.

As Rick stood up, he noticed a small corner of paper poking out from behind a piece of metal screwed to the wall behind the stove. He picked at it with his fingernail— a little more came into view. He wedged a twig between the metal and the wall, grasped the paper and pulled. Out came an old brown postcard.

"Hey, look at this! It's got writing on the back!"

Willow rushed over, and the two of them squinted at it in the poor light.

Maria looked at her watch. "Come on, you guys. We're gonna be late."

Rick shrugged and gave the postcard to Willow.

Kassim scrambled to his feet and brushed himself off.

"Yeah, let's boogie. If we're not back on time, Mr. Grantham will be on our backs for the rest of the week."

Willow jumped from the boxcar, made a pouch with the bottom of her T-shirt, and dropped the postcard and other clues into it. "Thanks, everyone."

"Too bad we didn't find more paintings, though," said Maria sadly.

Willow shrugged. "Didn't really expect to, but these clues are great."

"If they prove that a famous artist did your painting, you'll be rich," said Kassim eagerly. "You could buy a car!"

"Or a boat," suggested Maria.

"You could take us all to Disneyland," said Rick.

"Naw... let's fly to Hawaii and be beach bums," laughed Willow, and she and Maria started doing the hula.

"Hey, hold it."

Everyone stared at Rick. He looked uncomfortable. "I heard something weird. Are there really wolves or bears around here?"

"I don't think so." Kassim glanced warily at the forest shadows. "Why?"

"What's that?"

Petrified, the kids listened to a rustle approaching through the bushes. Closer... closer. Someone—or something—was on their trail.

With a manic yell, Kassim bolted, followed closely by Rick, Willow, and Maria.

The four musketeers tore down the trail and across the beach. They pushed out the boat and scrambled aboard. Kassim switched on the engine and flipped the throttle, and they shot off in a cloud of spray.

Behind them, three plump grouse resumed their steady march through the undergrowth.

Sketches and paintings

"The sketcher must seize one eternal moment, decide what to do, and put it down," said Arthur Lismer. A quick oil sketch allows an artist to capture that impression, perhaps a particular combination of light and landscape. Large oil paintings sometimes took months to finish, so the drawings and oil sketches done out in the Algoma forest were very important. The artists took their sketches home and used them as guides to create the bigger paintings.

The oil sketches were often made on standard boards — about the size of a small computer screen. They fitted into slots in a special box, so they could be transported without smudging the wet oil paint.

The sketches were sometimes exhibited with the finished paintings. In the Group's early days, the sketches sold better than the finished paintings because they were cheaper. People didn't want to spend much money on Canadian art, and many were not sure they liked the new style anyway.

www.utoronto.ca/gallery/lismer.htm
(shows the stages of one of Lismer's paintings from pencil sketch to finished canvas)

CHAPTER SEVEN

Late that evening, Maria and Willow sat in their pyjamas on Willow's bed.

"I wish we could go back to Kristo and get the sketch," Willow grumbled. "Sunday is ages away."

"Yup. No more free time is a bummer," agreed Maria. Then she brightened. "We could try to figure out those clues, though."

Willow pulled out a plastic bag and upended it, and Maria spread the objects over the bed.

Willow pounced on the piece of plate with the dried paint. "This definitely means an artist used the boxcar." She placed it to one side.

"But what about the other stuff," said Maria doubtfully. "It's just garbage."

"Garbage gives information," Willow said firmly. "All the best spies and private investigators check out the garbage." She poked the sardine tin. "So . . . what does this tell us?"

"That someone was hungry?"

Willow giggled. "No, really."

"Really?" Maria considered the tin again. "That someone liked sardines, and they ate them a long time ago, because the tin's nearly rusted away."

"OK. And the bottle?"

"They liked brandy."

"But was it the same person?"

"Who knows." Maria shrugged, then pointed to the faded label on the bottle. "Maybe a museum could trace the brand and when it was sold."

"There's one thing it does tell us ... " Willow looked mischievously at Maria. "The owner was probably a man."

Maria snickered.

"What about this?" Maria picked up the squished cigarette package. "It says Players Light. Gramps once told me that in the old days they didn't have tipped cigarettes. I don't think this package is very old."

"OK, let's forget about the cigarette pack and the sardine tin," agreed Willow. "But what about the postcard?"

The picture showed a row of old stone houses with "Sheffield" printed in one corner.

"Sheffield ... isn't that in England?" wondered Maria.

"Guess so, it's an English stamp," agreed Willow. "Some old king with a beard—Rick's got some like that in his collection."

"Why would anyone have a postcard on a boxcar

camping trip?" Maria asked. "They wouldn't get mail, would they?"

"Could have been used as a bookmark," suggested Willow. "That's how Dad uses them."

"But why was it behind that metal plate?"

"'Cause it fell out of the book ... and someone else picked it up ... and put it where the owner would see it." Willow finished triumphantly. "But it slipped down!"

"Oh boy, you've thought of everything," Maria teased. She turned the card over and tried to read the message.

Dear A and E,

Hope   keeping well
      show went well
Spring is here.   bluebells.
These cottages are like Uncle Albert's
place. Hugs   little Marjorie. Take
her   cinema to see The Kid.
We couldn't stop laughing. Letter
more time.

Constance

Mr. and Mrs. A.   er
69 Bedfor   Pl.
Toro
Canada

"The address must be Toronto, Canada," Maria added.
"Yep," Willow agreed. "Now we just have to find out"

which Group of Seven artist had the first initial 'A' and a last name that finished with 'er,' lived in Toronto at Bedfor-something... Place?—had a kid called Marjorie and an Uncle Albert, and knew someone called Constance who lived in Sheffield, England."

Maria rolled on her back, laughing hysterically. "Yeah, right. We're stuck in canoe camp in the middle of no-where; it's real easy to research stuff."

Willow chuckled. "Sure, it's easy. Thanks to the compu-ter, I think I already know."

Maria leaped up. "You do? Who?"

"Arthur Lismer. Want to see if we can prove it?"

Maria nodded eagerly.

The two girls sat in the dark looking at the glowing screen. Willow's fingers flew rapidly over the keyboard as she logged onto a site listing the Group of Seven members.

Maria bent forward clutching the postcard. She jabbed excitedly at the screen. "You're right...Arthur Lismer... he lived in Sheffield. This card must be from his family."

Willow smiled smugly. "Yup, now let's try something else." Her fingers flew again.

"The Kid, why are you putting that in?" Maria puzzled, then crowed with delight as the screen flickered and changed. "It's an old movie! They went to see a Charlie Chaplin movie called *The Kid*. Cool!" She looked solemnly at the postcard. "Wow. We're figuring out what people did years ago. Weird, eh?"

"Never mind that, look at the date."

>>>>>>>>>>>>>>>>>>>>>> **Arthur Lismer** <<<<<<<<<<<<<<<<<<<<

 Arthur Lismer suggested the name "the Group of Seven," and became one of its best-known members. He was born in the industrial city of Sheffield, England, in 1885. At thirteen, he won a scholarship to the local art school and later studied in Antwerp, Belgium. Lismer came to Canada in 1911 and met other artists who eventually became members of the Group. In 1912 he returned to England to marry, and he and his wife, Esther, settled in Toronto. Their little girl, Marjorie, was born in 1913.

Although he missed the first trips to Algoma, Lismer went frequently in the 1920s. He loved the forest and liked to dress as a lumberjack. Some of his most famous paintings, including *September Gale, Canadian Jungle, Forest Algoma* and *Isles of Spruce* are from his Algoma visits.

Although his work is now famous, Lismer's paintings sold modestly during his lifetime. He once joked that he had "the largest private collection of Lismers in Canada." Lismer died in Montreal in 1969.

www.tomthomson.org/frmal.htm
www.mcmichael.com/lismer.htm

"What date? I can't read the date on the postcard, it's smudged."

"No, the date of the movie." Willow pointed to the screen.

"See . . . 1921. The postcard date has to be the same year or just after."

" 'Cause they've just seen a new film," finished Maria excitedly. "Yes! If we can find out what date Lismer went on the painting trips, then everything really is connected."

The girls bent over the computer once more.

It was very late the same night. The village of MacCallum slumbered. Only one cottage had shafts of light peeking through the blinds. Kristo was working into the small hours of morning.

He laboured feverishly at a table covered with paints, a hair dryer, and a jar of dust. Willow's cleaned oil sketch glowed on the easel in front of him.

Kristo had found a cedar shingle and cut it to the same size as the sketch, rubbed it with dust and gently baked it in the oven until it looked like the old shingle. Now he was meticulously copying the oil sketch onto it.

The work went quickly and easily. He was used to copying Group of Seven styles. The vigorous brush strokes, the flow of paint, and the choice of colours were all second nature to him.

"Feels like a Lismer," Kristo muttered to himself as he finished. He propped his sketch beside the original and closely compared them while cleaning his brushes. Next, he moved over to his bookshelf, pushing several books aside before thumbing through one on Lismer.

He found half a dozen reproductions of paintings and sketches from the Algoma area and held them up, one at a time, against the original. Nothing matched exactly, but — wait! Excitedly, Kristo flipped back to a painting called *Forest Algoma 1922* . . . this was close and the dates fitted. He carefully checked. Yes, this sketch could be a very early version of a large painting he'd seen somewhere — yes, in the McMichael Gallery.

Kristo replaced the book and picked up the original oil sketch. He gloated over the pattern of bare tree trunks springing skyward beyond the rocky shoreline. "What a little beauty. At last . . . my own Group of Seven." He carefully placed it on the table and looked across at his copy with a sly grin.

"I'll use you, along with a really convincing story, for those rotten kids." He plucked his copy off the easel and peered closely at it. "Got to carefully age it," he muttered. "Good thing I've got a few days. It doesn't have to be perfect . . . just enough to fool them." He picked up the hair dryer to speed the drying of the paint.

>> Copies, pastiches, and forgeries <<

 Art students often copy famous paintings, because copying is one of the best ways to learn the techniques used by the original artist. But these copies are considered an art exercise and are rarely sold or shown in a gallery.

Many artists imitate the *styles* of other artists without copying a specific work. If the painting is a good one, it is regarded as being "of the school of" the original painter. Poorer-quality paintings in the style of another artist may be called "pastiches" or "tourist art."

A copy or pastiche sold as an original painting by a famous artist is a forgery. The artist may intend to create a fake or may sell it innocently to someone else, who adds a false signature. The buyer of the signed painting thinks he or she is purchasing a real work of art and pays a higher price for the painting than it is worth.

In the 1950s, as Group of Seven works increased in value, many forgeries appeared. Group of Seven members A.J. Casson, Arthur Lismer, and A.Y. Jackson helped the police detect forged works attributed to Group of Seven members. Casson alone found more than 300 fakes.

CHAPTER EIGHT

Finally it was Sunday morning; Camp Hiawatha was full of friends and family who had come to watch the final regatta.

"HI YA, MINNIE," came a voice over the loudspeaker.

"HIAWATHA," everyone roared back.

"Breakfast is served," continued the announcement, and the hungry crowd surged towards the outdoor kitchen, where pancakes were being snatched from the griddle as fast as they were cooked.

"Mom, Dad, when you watch the canoe races, I'm in the yellow canoe with Kassim," said Rick between bites. "We're gonna kick butt."

"Aren't you entering the races, Willow?" asked her mother, Shari Jennings.

"Naw... other than the relay, we're all in that—racing's not my thing. Be on the dock at ten though. That's when I demonstrate a rescue technique." She looked cockily across at her brother. "That's where *I* kick butt."

After the gigantic breakfast, everyone cheered for the races, demonstrations, and games. The campers—tanned, fit, and exuberant—loved showing off their new skills.

Rick and Kassim came first in the canoe races and Rick came second in the log-rolling contest. He pinned his ribbons around the peak of his cap, then jammed it on backwards. They fluttered furiously behind him every time he moved.

Willow was thrilled. Her rescue demonstration had gone well, and the crowd had cheered and applauded.

"I swear you've both grown," said Shari, giving them bear hugs. "And you're great canoeists."

"Hey, we should all enroll in a whitewater canoe camp next year. Then the whole family gets a wilderness adventure . . . We could film it!" Marty Forster proudly patted his kids' backs, then looked at his watch. "Get your gear, so we can load up the bus. It's a long drive back, and I'm looking at the first edit of my film tomorrow."

"Dad, we need to stop in the village on the way out. Rick and I have to pick up something at the artist's studio—near the car park."

"Is it important?" asked Marty. "It's hopeless trying to find a parking place for the bus on a weekend."

"It's really *really* important," Willow insisted. "We won't be long. We promise."

"She's right, Dad," Rick agreed. "It's something Willow found and if it's what we think it is, it will make an awesome story. You and Mom could definitely make a film about it."

"It all sounds very mysterious." Marty Forster grinned at his kids. "Well, I need to fill up with gas anyway. Can you go while I'm at the garage?"

Rick and Willow nodded and rushed off to say goodbye to their friends and to get their gear.

"Hey, have you seen that neat old school bus in the parking lot? It's made into a camper and has a gigantic whale painted on the side." Kassim rushed breathlessly into the boys' dorm.

Rick laughed. "Yeah, I've seen it—we live in it! And the whale's an orca."

Kassim gaped at him in astonishment. "What do you mean 'live in it?' Like, camp in it?"

Rick put down his sports bag. "No. We *live* in it. That's our home."

"I thought you lived on the west coast."

"We do. Mom and Dad's office and studio, Orca Enterprises, is in Vancouver. But they're filmmakers, so they're always travelling around. We live in the bus and go with them."

"What about school?"

"We take correspondence courses. If we're in a place for a while, we register for classes in stuff we like. Willow's been taking art classes while we've been in Toronto, and I joined a baseball team instead."

"What about a phone?"

"Cell phone."

"TV?"

"When we're hooked up to an electrical outlet."

"Computers?"

"Yup, battery-run laptops."

"Bathroom?"

"No bathroom, we go in the bushes." Rick kept a straight face, then punched Kassim's arm. "Idiot, 'course we've got a bathroom. It's just tiny, like in a camper."

Kassim shook his head and laughed. "Kind of a whacko lifestyle. No school, eh? I could live with that."

"Want to see inside the bus?"

"Sure!" said Kassim. "Here, I'll give you a hand." He grabbed a bag.

Rick pulled on his backpack, grabbed his life jacket with one hand and a plastic bag full of laundry with the other. They walked to the parking lot.

Maria and Willow were exchanging phone numbers and addresses.

"Must be exciting travelling around like that," said Maria wistfully. "I've hardly been anywhere."

Willow shrugged as she zipped up her backpack. "Sometimes it's OK, but I don't have many friends." She looked across at Maria. "I'll miss you."

The two girls smiled, then tearfully hugged each other.

"Remember we're coming to the AGO with you if we can," said Maria.

Willow nodded.

"And don't forget to phone and tell me what happens with Kristo!"

Willow laughed. "I'll phone when we're in Toronto. It's been awful not being able to get to Kristo's now that we think the sketch is for real. Come on. I can show you the bus before we leave."

Willow dashed anxiously up the street to the studio, followed by Rick. "I can't wait to see the sketch again. I hope Kristo knows what he's doing. I shouldn't have left it."

"Can it, sis. It'll be fine." Rick reassured her as they went through the studio gate.

"Ah, good afternoon," said Kristo genially. "I wondered when you would turn up. Had a good week at camp?"

"Yes, thank you," replied Willow hurriedly. "Could we please have our painting? We don't have much time."

"Of course, of course. Now, do you want the good news or the bad?"

Willow's eyes widened. She said nothing.

Kristo picked up a plastic bag from the display cabinet, slid the painting out, and handed it to Willow. "The good news is that it's turned out nicely—hasn't it? I lightly cleaned the surface. It's really brightened up the colours." He laughed self-consciously. "It almost seems freshly done."

75

Willow looked at it closely, then back at Kristo and smiled. "Thanks, it looks great."

"What's the bad news?" Rick asked suspiciously.

Kristo turned serious. "I'm sorry to disappoint you, but I'm afraid it's not a Group of Seven." He paused. "What's more, I'm afraid the boxcar you found isn't genuine either."

"What do you mean? The colour was right... and the numbers—you—" Willow stopped, not wanting to reveal they'd followed him.

Kristo nodded sadly. "Yes, I'm sure everything was right, the colour, the numbers on the side, the interior—everything."

"Then what's wrong?" asked Willow, puzzled.

Kristo shrugged and spread his hands. "It was an elaborate joke."

Rick and Willow looked confused.

"I don't get it," Willow said flatly.

"It all started thirty years ago," Kristo explained, "when MacCallum began to grow. I asked some of the older villagers about the boxcar last night, and they remembered the story. Apparently an amateur artist found the abandoned boxcar in the 1960s. He and a group of artist friends used it for sketching—copying the Group of Seven's idea. They painted it and printed the numbers on the side. Then they built the bunks and installed a stove so they could camp out. It was all done in fun, a sort of

Group of Seven clubhouse. Everyone in the village knew about it. Then the group got older and moved away or died, and the boxcar was forgotten."

"That explains the cigarette pack," Rick muttered to Willow.

"But—but—the painting?" stammered Willow.

Kristo shrugged again. "I guess it was done by one of the artists. It's a nice little sketch though."

Willow's disappointment was a sharp pain in the gut. She could barely speak. She blindly passed the painting to Rick, her eyes misting over. "Thanks . . . for cleaning . . . for your trouble."

"It's OK," said Kristo. "I'm sorry to disappoint you . . . I was disappointed, too. You really had me going. I thought you'd found something special."

Willow rushed out of the studio so Kristo wouldn't see her crying. She had been so sure, and now she just felt stupid . . . and all that detective work—how could she be so wrong?

Willow ran down the street to the garage, bolted onto the bus, into her bedroom, and slammed the door.

Back at the studio, Rick shrugged. "Oh well, I never thought it was that good anyway, but I guess we'll keep it."

Kristo looked uneasy. "It's not worth much. I'll buy it from you if you like. I could probably sell it to a tourist."

"I know, but Willow really liked it. I think she'll want to have it." Rick added, "I'll give it to her for her birthday."

Kristo reluctantly handed over the sketch. "You're the last of the big spenders, young man," he joked clumsily.

"Thanks." Rick turned to go, then paused in the door-way. "Did *you* ever go to the boxcar?"

"No, I've never seen it," Kristo answered. "Maybe I'll hike out there some day."

"Maybe . . . . well, bye," said Rick. He left, the picture under his arm.

Kristo walked to the garden gate and watched as Rick ran down the street to the garage and boarded the bus.

Slowly the bus pulled out and headed towards the highway, leaving a faint haze of blue smoke hanging in the air.

Kristo let out his breath in a long, slow sigh of relief.

Rick ran breathlessly up to the big blue school bus and leapt aboard.

"Where's Willow?" he demanded.

His mom gestured to the bedroom partition. "Did you two fight?"

"No," said Rick, looking offended. He made his way down the bus and pounded on Willow's door.

"Come on, Willow. Come out. Don't be upset—Kristo's lying."

"Seats, everyone. Time to roll." Marty swung into the driver's seat and the doors closed with a puff.

Rick plopped down on the bench and placed the painting in the middle of the table. Willow came out of her bedroom and slid in beside him, still looking puffy-eyed.

"He's lying, Willow. I think he made the whole thing up. I asked him if he'd ever been to the boxcar—he said no!"

The real thing?

How do you recognize a genuine painting? History, science, and art can all be helpful.

The history of a painting can often be traced through records, from the time it left the hands of the artist to its most recent owner. But some paintings have adventures—they are bought and sold, stolen and recovered, and even carried off during wars—so their history is not available.

Scientific techniques can identify the source and age of a picture, sometimes exposing fakes. Some supposed Group of Seven paintings were on Japanese plywood, which was not available when the pictures are supposed to have been painted. Chemical analysis of tiny pieces of pigments may also help—a supposed Tom Thomson painting had used titanium oxide, which only came into use more than a decade after his death.

Art experts study the work of individual painters, which helps them recognize other works by the same artist.

Although these methods can't always prove who the artist was, they make it possible to identify many forgeries by showing who the artist *wasn't*. Occasionally, though, experts—in history, science, and art—don't agree. The authenticity of some famous paintings is still controversial.

http://www.triangle-st.com/forgery/
(tests your skills in detecting forgeries)

CHAPTER NINE

The bus bumped and barrelled over the potholes. The northern road ran through rugged country and needed all of Marty Forster's concentration. He sighed with frustration as he hit yet another bump and the old bus squeaked and rattled in protest. The noise was making it difficult for him to hear his family's conversation.

He drove up the next hill and pulled into a viewpoint at the top.

"OK," Marty said, putting on the brakes. "This is killing me . . . I can only hear every fourth word of this convoluted story. I'd like to see the picture that's causing all the trouble."

He slid his long legs from behind the wheel, stood up and plucked the oil sketch from the table. "Nice. It *does* look like a Group of Seven. Someone's done a good job. Now what's the problem?"

Shari filled him in.

"Don't be disappointed, Willow, it's still a great story." He gave her a hug.

"But why did Kristo lie?" Willow asked. "He had no reason to lie about going to see the boxcar."

Rick agreed. "Yeah, it doesn't compute."

Shari looked at the painting again. "Look, kids, I hate to say this when you're so gung-ho, but think about it logically. A boxcar painted up as a clubhouse is far more believable than the real one complete with a genuine painting." She looked searchingly across at her children. "Isn't it?"

Rick and Willow reluctantly nodded.

"Maybe Kristo was feeling foolish...he'd rushed out to see it. He did believe it was real until he talked to the villagers. Perhaps he lied because he didn't want to let on he'd been sucked into believing the improbable, by a couple of kids."

Marty, his arm still around Willow's shoulder, gave her another squeeze. "Cheer up. Take the painting to the AGO anyway. Show it to the teacher and see how good he thinks it is. I guarantee he's got a hundred and one interesting stories about people thinking they've found a Group of Seven, and your story's a dilly. I bet no one else has seen a replica of the boxcar."

Shari picked up the sketch and held it against the partition. "We should frame it. It's a nice memento of our foray into northern Ontario. What do you think, Willow?"

Willow glumly took the painting and looked at it again. "Dunno...maybe...I'll show it to my teacher first."

Marty yawned and stretched and climbed behind the wheel again. "On to Toronto. Let's keep rolling or we'll never make it."

As the bus rumbled down the highway, Rick and Willow sprawled on Willow's bunk, examining the plastic bag of clues.

"Mom and Dad believe Kristo's story." Willow sighed.

Rick shrugged. "It's convincing, for sure. But they never met him. We have. We know he's a weirdo."

"Mom said be logical, so let's be logical. What does all this really prove?"

"Not much," said Rick honestly.

"Except this." Willow held up the postcard. "Kristo's story explains everything except this." She sat up and jabbed excitedly at the card. 'A' something 'er.' Fits with Arthur Lismer. My art teacher has a book about him. I bet we can find out more about his family, and his address."

"But if the boxcar was set up by artists in the 1960s, why would this postcard be for Lismer? Wasn't he dead by then?"

Willow suddenly looked at Rick with a brilliant smile. "You've got it, Rick Forster...that's it."

Rick looked at her blankly.

Willow spoke slowly. "The postcard *is* older than the 1960s." She passed it to Rick.

Rick peered at it and tried to make out the blurred

postmark. "It says . . . nineteen twenty something . . . And the stamp's King George V. So what?"

"So, it was found *behind* the metal plate. How would it get there if the stove wasn't put in till the sixties?" Willow bounced excitedly on the bed. "No matter what, we should check out the postcard. I can't wait to see my art teacher."

Unconvinced, Rick left Willow's room and lay on his own bunk, staring at the ceiling. Willow had really got herself in a state over the boxcar. He didn't know what to believe. *I don't trust Kristo,* he thought. *He's a real grease ball . . . Yeah, Crisco the grease ball—I'll tell Willow that one. But if Kristo's story is true, why did he lie about visiting the boxcar?*

The bus eased onto a smoother highway. As the bumping and rattling gave way to the normal hum of wheels on pavement, Willow and Rick drifted off to sleep.

A few days later, Willow, Rick, Maria, and Kassim tiptoed into the back of the basement art room at the Art Gallery of Ontario. Willow waved wildly to catch the eye of her art teacher, Jay Kemp. A class was in progress and the room was full of students quietly concentrating on their work.

Jay waved back and motioned for her to come in. Willow pointed to her friends, and Jay nodded in welcome.

The kids tiptoed in, looking around curiously. In the middle of the room was a small stage set with a folding screen. A colourful piece of fabric hung from the screen down to a table covered with interesting objects.

>>>>>>>>**The Art Gallery of Ontario**<<<<<<<

 The Art Gallery of Ontario (AGO) has been in central Toronto since 1900. Originally named the Art Gallery of Toronto, it showed the first exhibition of the Group of Seven in 1920. Despite public criticism and lack of funds, the AGO has held many other exhibits of works by the Group and its individual members.

Now the AGO is home to one of the major collections of Group of Seven works. It is a wonderful place to see their paintings, because of its interactive exhibits. You can sit in a booth, put on headphones and listen to a curator teach you how to "take a walk through a picture," so you *really* see it.

Many Group of Seven sketches are exhibited near the finished paintings for easy comparison. There are also drawing stations where you can try sketching for yourself. Arthur Lismer was a great supporter of the AGO. He started the first children's art classes there, so Willow was attending a school Lismer had begun.

www.ago.on.ca

"It's still-life class," whispered Willow as they walked behind the silent semicircle of students.

Rick looked at Willow with new respect. "Are your classes like this?" he hissed.

"Yes," whispered Willow, surprised.

"Wow, you *must* be good. It's a real art school. No wonder you know all that Group of Seven stuff."

Willow rolled her eyes and made her way to Jay. She quietly introduced Rick and her friends, then handed Jay a padded envelope.

"What's this?" Jay asked. "A late birthday card or an early Christmas card?"

Willow smothered a chuckle. "No, just something I want you to see. What do you think?"

Jay slid the oil sketch out of the envelope. "Nice." He carried it over to an easel, set it down and looked at it from a distance. "Very nice. Who did it?"

The kids grinned as Willow whispered mysteriously, "That's the million–dollar question. Any ideas?"

Everyone leaned in anxiously to hear the answer.

Jay concentrated on the oil sketch, shrugged, then turned to the children. "I know what you'd like me to say, Willow, but I can't. I need to know the whole story before I call in someone else more qualified to give an opinion."

He looked at the four friends' excited faces and relented. "OK, OK … give me the dirt … how in hades did you get hold of an oil sketch in the style of the Group of Seven?"

Just as Willow was about to explain, the classroom door opened and a smartly dressed older man made his way over to them.

"Jay, have you got a minute?" The man stopped abruptly and went to look at the oil sketch. "What's this doing here?"

>>>>>>> **Arthur Lismer—art teacher** <<<<<<

 Arthur Lismer enjoyed children and was a pioneer in art education in Canada. When he began his work, public schools taught only "technique"—the skills students would need if they were going to become professional artists. These classes produced what Lismer called a "sad array of little sheets of colour studies."

Lismer believed that art should be fun and was about more than just technique. He felt that classes should "teach children to use their eyes and become aware of the beauty around them." He began Saturday morning classes for children in the Toronto and Montreal art museums. He encouraged the crowds of eager students to express their own ideas. Photos of his AGO classes show children sprawled across the floor creating a variety of art.

Lismer took art by children seriously and organized exhibitions of their painting to show adults what kids could do. He also taught older students at art colleges—many of his students became art teachers or artists themselves.

Jay pointed to Willow. "One of my students just brought it in."

"That's odd." The man swung around to Willow. "Did the McMichael Gallery send it down? They didn't say anything to me."

Everyone looked at him blankly.

"The oil sketch. It was brought into the McMichael. I went up to Kleinburg yesterday afternoon to examine it. Could be very exciting. But what is it doing here?"

CHAPTER TEN

The next few moments were a babble of explanations.

"Just a minute—this obviously needs time." The man held his hand up and the voices died down.

"Jay, when does your class finish?"

Jay looked at his watch. "Another forty minutes."

"OK, meet us in the boardroom." The man grabbed the painting and swept the four friends before him, up the stairs, and into his office. He placed the painting on the table and motioned for them to take seats.

He smiled. "I'm sorry, I haven't introduced myself. I'm Peter Reece, Chief Curator at the AGO. Now who's going to tell me about this?"

"Willow," chorused Rick, Maria, and Kassim.

Willow blushed furiously.

"OK, Willow. Tell me everything."

Willow held back nothing. She described discovering the boxcar, then the painting. She explained how she felt it might be a Group of Seven, so she took it to show Kristo.

Mr. Reece smiled when he heard about the spying, but listened intently as Willow recounted their second trip to the boxcar.

"This is so embarrassing," she said at one point, so Rick—with assistance from Kassim—described scaring Kristo away.

Willow then told how they gathered the clues.

"Those clues, do you still have them?" interrupted Mr. Reece.

Rick lifted up the plastic bag he'd been carrying and tipped them out on the table.

Mr. Reece gave a sigh of satisfaction. "So what happened next?"

Willow pointed to Rick. "He should tell you the next bit."

Rick described Kristo returning the painting to them, and how he caught Kristo out in the Big Lie. Then Willow shared what she and Maria had discovered on the Web. "But the Web's frustrating," she admitted. "I couldn't find everything I needed. Only little bits of information. It all needs checking out properly."

Mr. Reece agreed sympathetically, then lapsed into a long silence while the children wriggled uneasily on their chairs. Finally he took a deep breath. "Willow, have you looked at this oil sketch a lot?"

Willow flushed again. "Hundreds of times," she admitted. "I really like it."

"If I placed it beside an identical one, would you know which was the one you found?"

"I . . . I dunno." She shuffled uncomfortably. "Probably not if it was a good copy," she said honestly.

"Bet you could from the back," interrupted Rick. "Remember getting mad at me?"

Mr. Reece, Kassim, and Maria exchanged blank looks.

Willow stared at Rick for a second, then whooped. "Of course, I'd forgotten about your face!" she said.

"Me too," said Rick, and he turned the board over to show what he meant.

The tiny face wasn't there.

It was still fairly early the next morning when Mr. Reece's car swung by the Orca Enterprises bus to pick up Willow, Rick, the clues, and the oil sketch. They were going to compare both sketches at the McMichael Gallery in Kleinburg, about an hour's drive away.

"Nervous?" Mr. Reece asked.

"I wish Kristo wasn't coming," Willow admitted. "He's going to be mad when he sees us."

"He's going to be in trouble if your story checks out," said Mr. Reece. "He could be accused of forgery and theft." He fiddled in his pocket and handed a piece of paper to Willow. "I thought you might like to see this."

Willow and Rick read it carefully.

Esther and Arthur Lismer
69 Bedford Park Avenue
Toronto

Daughter Marjorie born 1913
Arthur had a sister named Constance who lived in
Sheffield, England.

In 1921 Charlie Chaplin's movie The Kid *was*
released and became very popular.

Lismer was in Algoma in 1921.

He often took along a bottle of brandy to "keep out
the chill."

Willow's smile stretched from ear to ear. "So the post-card really was sent to Lismer."

"Looks like it." Mr. Reece's eyes smiled back in the rear-view mirror. "I did some research last night. Your gut feeling was right. You're great detectives."

Rick bounced up and down excitedly. "That means the boxcar *was* real and the painting *is* a Group of Seven. Kristo lied about it all!"

"Hold on, hold on," Mr. Reece cautioned. "All it suggests is that the postcard was once sent to Lismer...nothing else. Kristo's sixties story could still be true—maybe someone collected old postcards. Besides, the postcard doesn't prove that Lismer painted the sketch."

"Oh." Deflated, Rick leaned back, then sat up again. "Not all of Kristo's story is true. We've pretty much proved he's a forger."

The two sketches stood side by side on easels in the McMichael's lab.

"They really *are* identical," Willow said in amazement. "I only know the right-hand one is the one we've just given you because I saw you put it there."

The McMichael's curator, Juliette Lefevre, gently lifted up the left-hand sketch. "This one has been in our care several days. We've already confirmed that it has all the characteristics of a Group of Seven oil sketch. So, shall we check the back?"

She turned the oil sketch over. There was the tiny knot-hole with two pencilled eyes and a mouth, an impish little face laughing up at them.

"Yessss!" Rick and Willow double slapped each other's palms. Then they turned to the two curators. "Now what?"

Juliette checked her watch. "Kristo should be arriving soon. Why don't you both wait in the back room until we need you."

Kristo strode confidently through the trees towards the entrance of the McMichael. It was a beautiful gallery overlooking a deep wooded river valley. He paused to admire the polar bear sculpture by the front doors and jokingly saluted the security guard. "I'm Kristo. I've got an appointment with Juliette Lefevre."

The security guard looked at him oddly and punched in a phone number. "He's here." He replaced the phone and pointed down the hall. "You can go through, sir."

This is it, thought Kristo jubilantly. *For once in my life something big's happening. With the boxcar and the oil sketch, my name will be forever associated with the Group of Seven.*

He knocked sharply on the door, entered the lab, and saw Juliette talking animatedly to an unfamiliar man.

"Good afternoon, Kristo," Juliette broke off her conversation. "This is Peter Reece from the AGO."

The two men shook hands.

"We have something very interesting to show you."

Juliette and Mr. Reece moved to one side to reveal the two easels and two identical oil sketches.

Kristo felt an iron hand clench his throat, and the air squeezed out of his lungs. Something had gone massively wrong. He forced himself to breathe normally.

"Goodness." His voice came out at a slightly higher pitch. He decided to try a light approach. "Where did the other one come from? Your collection?"

No one said anything, so he made a pretense of peering closer. "Which one's mine?"

"We were rather hoping you could shed some light on that," Mr. Reece rumbled.

There was a long silence as Kristo looked from one person to the other. "Is something wrong?" he asked.

As if in response, Willow and Rick entered the lab and walked over to stand beside Mr. Reece.

"You two—How did you—?"

Kristo lost it.

His eyes wildly scanned the lab looking for an escape. "If I can't have it, no one can," he whispered, grabbing at the sketch and sending both easels crashing to the ground. Kristo turned swiftly on his heels and ran through the door, through the gallery, and blindly past the security guard.

"Get him!" Rick sprinted for the door.

Juliette grabbed the phone and gabbled instructions to security.

"Willow, stay put!" bellowed Mr. Reece as he followed Rick down the hall.

"No way!" muttered Willow, joining in the chase.

Within seconds, curators, lab technicians, and security staff were in hot pursuit, with Rick leading the pack.

A busload of tourists gasped as Kristo, closely followed by Rick, ran through the entrance, around the corner of the building, and down the nearest trail.

"Which way did they go?" yelled the security guard. An elderly visitor pointed to the trail.

Kristo pounded along the path, heart racing. It was no good, the kid was still chasing him. In sheer desperation, he leapt over the low railings and crashed through the woods towards the river valley.

"Let me, son," the security guard called, but Rick hopped over the barrier and followed Kristo.

Groaning, the security guard followed.

Staff and visitors lined the barrier to watch the action.

Willow elbowed through the crowd and stood beside Mr. Reece and Juliette. All eyes were riveted on the scene below.

Kristo slipped and stumbled through the trees and bushes, causing a trail of small avalanches. Rick slithered behind him. Suddenly Kristo sprinted to the riverbank. At the same time, Rick grabbed an overhanging branch and launched himself through the air.

"*GERONIMO!*" yelled Rick.

The rest seemed to happen in slow motion.

Rick crash-landed on Kristo's back. They fell forward and rolled towards the river.

The security guard leapt out of the bushes and pinned Kristo's arm to the ground.

The spectators all sucked in their breath as the sketch jolted from Kristo's hand, sailed through the air, and landed in the tumbling water.

"No! no!" sobbed Willow.

Horrified, the kids and curators watched helplessly as

the board was swept over a waterfall and dashed against a jagged rock. The shattered pieces drifted off downstream.

A subdued group reassembled in the lab after Kristo had been escorted into a police car. It had been a long afternoon.

Rick sported a bandage over one eye and scratches across his face.

Juliette blew her nose hard and gestured towards the remaining oil sketch. "Willow, perhaps you and Rick would like this as a souvenir when all the formalities are concluded." She smiled tremulously at them. "And, rest assured, we will check out the boxcar, so something good may still come of this sad affair."

Willow picked up the painting and looked at it wistfully. "I like this, but knowing it was done by Kristo . . . I'm not sure—" She turned it over, then stopped and stared. She looked up at everyone, eyes dancing.

"Juliette! It's—" Almost speechless, Willow pointed to the back of the sketch. "Kristo—he took the wrong one!"

From the knothole, a mischievous face smiled back at all of them.

Imagine collecting so many paintings you have to build a special house for them. Robert McMichael and his wife, Signe, did just that. They were passionate collectors of Canadian art.

The McMichaels started collecting paintings by members of the Group of Seven in the 1950s. They hunted down pictures that were privately owned and bought as many as they could afford. They built a house to hold the paintings, on the edge of a lovely wooded valley near Kleinburg, on the northern outskirts of Toronto.

In 1965, the McMichaels donated their house and all the paintings to the Ontario government as a public gallery, but they continued buying Canadian art and donating it to the collection. The McMichael Canadian Art Collection now contains many works by the Group of Seven and other Canadian artists, as well as important collections of First Nations prints, paintings and sculpture.

Several members of the Group of Seven, including Arthur Lismer, are buried on the grounds of the gallery. Big beautiful rocks from their beloved Canadian wilderness mark their graves. They'd approve of that.

www.mcmichael.com

AUTHORS' NOTE

This story is a work of fiction based on some real background. The artists who eventually became members of the Group of Seven took painting trips into northern Ontario in a boxcar. We wondered what had happened to the boxcar and discovered that it had long since been destroyed.

Immediately we began playing the "what if?" game in our imaginations. What if... the boxcar still existed? What if... a couple of kids found it? What if... there was an old forgotten sketch inside it? And so our story grew.

There are several real places in our story. The Algoma Central Railway still exists, and every year tourists ride up to the beautiful northern wilderness to see where the Group of Seven painted. But we invented Camp Hiawatha and the small town of MacCallum. We didn't want any artists in the real communities to be confused with Kristo! In fact, all the people in our story are fictional characters. We do, however, refer to several Group of Seven artists, particularly Arthur Lismer. Information about them is authentic.

The Art Gallery of Ontario and the McMichael Canadian Art Collection exist and are wonderful places to see Group of Seven paintings. The Lismer painting mentioned in our story, *Forest Algoma 1922,* can be seen at the McMichael. Unfortunately, the sketch Willow and Rick found, like the postcard and the boxcar, exists only within the story.

So what else is factual? Everything in the boxes. The Web sites we have listed are all current at the time of publication, but be aware that Web sites sometimes change without notice and new sites appear constantly. However, we are confident that you keen Internet users will be able to find similar information using keywords from the boxes as a guide.

Willow and Rick, though fictional characters, have taken a strong hold on our imaginations. Watch for their next adventure, where they visit the *S. S. Moyie,* an old sternwheeler beached beside B.C.'s Kootenay Lake, and meet a young woman searching for a lost silver mine.

—*Andrea and David Spalding*

ABOUT THE AUTHORS

Andrea and David Spalding live on Pender Island, British Columbia. They spent many years performing stories and folk music in Canadian schools, and are now full-time writers. Their children are grown, giving them freedom to travel across Canada and write about their discoveries.

Andrea has written eight books for children, including *Finders Keepers, An Island of My Own, Phoebe and the Gypsy, Sarah May and the New Red Dress,* and *Me and Mr. Mah.* Her books for adults include biographies, cookbooks, and guidebooks.

David has written, co-written, or edited ten books. Most are about science for adults, with recent books on dinosaurs and whales. He has also written short stories and radio programs and contributed to encyclopedias and textbooks.

For more information about the Spaldings, check out their Web site at www.gulfislands.com/spalding/.